Night Job

Night

Job

Karen Hesse

illustrated by G. Brian Karas

Candlewick Press

On Friday nights, when the sun goes down,
I snap the clips shut on Dad's lunch box
and climb onto the back of his bike.

ONLY

We zoom over the darkening bay,
riding the dusky highway.

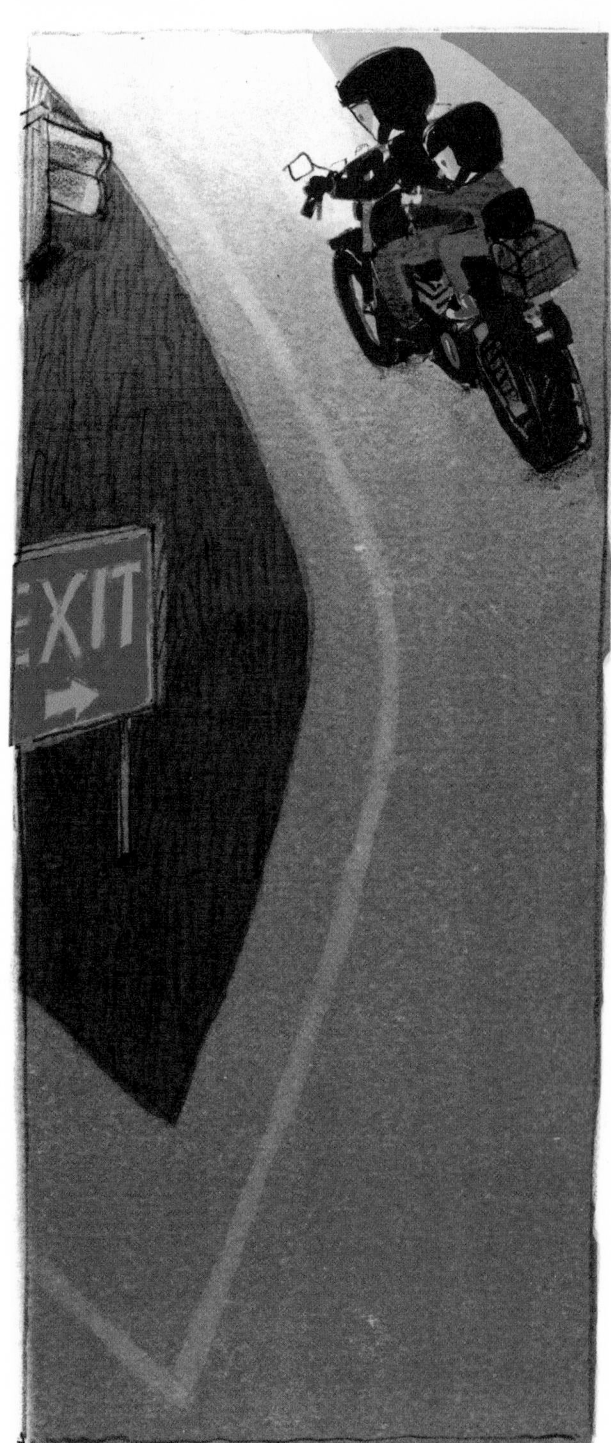

For a while the air stinks of old fish,

but at the school, it smells like lilacs.

We pull into our space.
Dad hauls out a ring of keys
as big as the rising moon.
He opens the door,
and the building sighs.
Come, it whispers to us.

We start in the gym,
flipping on the first and
last in the row of switches.

I shoot baskets in the half-light,
the ball bouncing in time with
the *shoosh* of Dad's broom.

Our radio travels with us from room to room.
We scrub the cafeteria, then sweep the stage
while listening to a game played miles away,

where the sun is shining on an emerald field
in a stadium filled with people eating
hot dogs and peanuts and drinking lemonade.

We tack back and forth down the hallway,
sweeping the school from stem to stern.

At ten Dad leads the way to the courtyard,
where we unwrap our egg salad sandwiches,
with their triple dollop of mayo
and a heaping teaspoon of chopped pickle.
We take big bites that fill our mouths and chew
and chew
and chew

until there are only crumbs left.
And then we chew those, too.

As Dad polishes the library,
I stretch out on the green vinyl sofa

and read aloud to him
until I fall asleep.

It's four in the morning when Dad wakes me
and helps me into my jacket.
We close the door behind us.

The cool air jolts us awake
as we roar toward home.

Deer startle.
A skunk raises its tail . . .

but Dad revs his bike and we fly over the
brightening bay, the two of us airborne,
hooting, making the fishermen
shake their heads and frown.

Dad shifts into neutral half a block from home
and we glide, silently, into our spot.

The sky lightens and Dad yawns.
I head to the kitchen to clean out Dad's lunch box.

By the time the sun bursts out of the sea,
Dad has nodded off in the big recliner.
Come, the chair whispers.

I climb up beside Dad
and soon we are drifting away together . . .

riding a watery highway
on a rising swell of dreams.